Contents

First Published 2001 by Brown Watson
The Old Mill, 76 Fleckney Road,
Kibworth Beauchamp,
Leicestershire LE8 0HG

© 2001 Brown Watson, England
Reprinted 2005
ISBN: 0-7097-1340-1
Printed in China

easy to read
farm stories

Illustrated by Lawrie Taylor
Stories by Maureen Spurgeon

Brown Watson
ENGLAND

The Little Donkey

Daisy Donkey was not at all dainty. She was big and clumsy, with bald patches on her coat. She had been called Daisy by Ken, a man at the animal shelter. 'Daisy has been badly treated,' he told Farmer Green.

'Could your Tom and Katie look after her?'
'Please, Dad!' cried Tom.
'Please!' added Katie. 'Daisy really needs a good home!'
Farmer Green nodded. 'She can stay on our farm,' he said. 'You can look after her!'

Tom and Katie were very glad! Daisy loved being on the farm. She would wait by the gate for them to get home from school. Then she would bend her head for them to scratch her long ears.

But she jumped at the slightest sound! If one of the farm dogs barked, or the cockerel crowed, or if a noisy lorry went past, Daisy would bray in fright!
'Hee-haw! HEE-HAW!'

'No need to be frightened,' said Katie. She
stroked Daisy along her back.
'Daisy was frightened by something which
made a loud noise,' said Ken. 'She cannot
forget it.'

The days became longer. Katie and Tom found a rug, a bridle and a saddle for Daisy. They put on riding hats and took turns to ride the little donkey and lead her around the meadow.

'It is lucky that Daisy came to your farm,'
Ken said. 'Our shelter was too small for her
to stay for long.'
'Can't you make the animal shelter bigger?'
asked Katie.

'We cannot afford it!' said Ken. 'But we are hoping to make some money at the Town Show next Saturday! Will you come and buy something from our stall?'

'You know we will!' said Katie.

Help Ferndale
Animal Shelter
at the
Town Show

'I do wish we could help some more!' said Tom thoughtfully.

They both began to think hard. Daisy wanted to help too, nuzzling them with her long nose.

'I know!' said Katie at last. 'Let's wear some big posters saying – PLEASE HELP THE ANIMAL SHELTER – and take Daisy to the show! She can carry a tin to collect the money!'

'Good idea!' said Tom.

'Hee-haw!' cried Daisy. But this time, she was braying because she knew Tom and Katie were pleased! 'Hee-haw!'

They ran to see what their Mum and Dad
thought of the idea.
'Let me find some big pieces of paper for
the posters!' said Mum. Then she made a
slot in a toffee tin to put money inside.

Tom and Katie worked hard, drawing and painting the posters. Then, two posters were threaded on string, so that one poster would be at the front and the other at the back.

Farmer Green hung the collecting tin carefully around Daisy's neck. 'Put on your riding hat, Tom,' he said. 'You can ride Daisy to the show with Katie leading her!'

Daisy felt pleased with herself, and very proud. All along the way to the show, people came up and stroked and patted her, wanting to know about the animal shelter.

They put money in the collecting tin, too!
'Hee-haw!' cried Daisy each time a coin
clattered into the tin. Katie held the leading
rein firmly. 'It is all right, Daisy,' said Tom.
'It is all right.'

Children were blowing up balloons and making them go pop! 'Hee-haw!' brayed Daisy in fright. Then a drum sounded. 'Boom-BOOM!'

'HEE-HAW!' went Daisy, louder still.

A line of horses with bells and ribbons went past Daisy.
CRACK! Their trainer cracked her whip on the ground. She was telling the horses to turn a corner. CRACK! CRACK!

'HEE-HAW!' Daisy had never brayed quite so loudly. 'HEE-HAW! HEE-HAW!' She began to trot and then to run and then to gallop!

'Stop, Daisy!' shouted Tom. 'Please, stop!'

'Hee-haw! HEE-HAW!' It seemed to Tom that lots of other donkeys were joining in! He held on to Daisy with all his might! He wanted to shut his eyes tight, hardly daring to look up.

'Stop, young man!' someone shouted. 'You can stop now!'

'Hurrah!' someone else shouted. 'It's the donkey from the animal shelter! The one we saw on the road!'

Tom felt a strong arm around his back. A hand pulled gently at Daisy's bridle and Ken's calm voice spoke into her long ears. 'It's all right, Daisy. It's all right!'

Tom looked up at last, not feeling at all happy. 'Sorry, Ken,' he began. 'We wanted to raise money for the animal shelter, but...' 'And so you have!' Ken told him.

He gave a grin and waved a handful of money at Tom. 'Look! First prize for winning the Donkey Derby! And people are still giving us money! You and Daisy have done us proud!'

How Daisy enjoyed being stroked and patted and told what a clever donkey she was! 'We're proud of you, Daisy,' said Katie. 'Lucky for us that you came to live on our farm!'

Ben and Rosy

Ben and Rosy were two big, strong horses. They had worked at Hill Farm for a long, long time. 'Your Grandad had Ben and Rosy when I was a boy,' Farmer West told his children, Jack and Susan. 'Hill Farm would not be quite the same without them!'

'But,' he went on, 'they are getting old and they are getting slow. I think it is time that we made some changes at Hill Farm!'
Jack and Susan looked at each other. What did their dad mean?

They soon found out! One morning there came a loud 'BEEP! BEEP!' and two big, black wheels and something shiny and red appeared! 'Dad has bought a tractor!' shouted Susan.

'And Mum is driving it!' added Jack. They stopped feeding the chickens and went to get a closer look. Mum and Dad looked very pleased. The tractor looked so bright and cheerful!

'Meet Toby the tractor!' Mum said. 'He can pull a plough, clear a ditch, tow a trailer, move heavy loads...'
'But Ben and Rosy do all that!' said Susan. 'What work will they do?'

'They can have a rest!' said Dad. 'The tractor can do their work in half the time!' That was true. With the tractor it was possible to plough a field, dig a ditch and put up a fence in one day!

And the tractor still looked bright and cheerful, not at all tired!
'Good old Toby the tractor!' said the farmer.
He even gave the tractor's front wheel a pat, just like he used to pat Ben and Rosy!

'It seems very strange for us not to be working on the farm,' Ben said to Rosy.
'I do not like it,' Rosy said to Ben. 'With no work for us to do, there is no need for the farmer to keep us here!'

'No need to talk like that!' said Ben. 'Toby
the tractor cannot do everything!'
But Rosy shook her big head sadly.
'It seems to me,' she said, 'there is nothing
that tractor cannot do!'

This time, Ben said nothing. He had a horrible feeling that Rosy might be right. How long would the farmer be able to let them stay if the tractor was doing their work?

Ben lifted his big head up to the sky.
'Let us go into our stable,' he said. 'It looks
like rain.' Rosy stamped her big hooves.
She tried not to look at Farmer West
working with the tractor again.

'That is all the planting done!' Farmer West called to his wife. 'Just in time before a spell of bad weather, too! And it's all thanks to our new tractor!' He just managed to lock up the shed as rain began to fall.

It rained all night long. Ben and Rosy heard it beating down on the roof of their stable. Early next day, the door opened and in came Jack and Susan in their rain-hats and wellington boots.

'Hello, Ben and Rosy,' said Jack.
'Here are your oats and some hay,' said
Susan. But before Ben and Rosy had begun
to eat, there came a loud cry from the yard
outside.

'Come along, Toby!' cried Farmer West. 'We have work to do! The rain has washed away so much soil from Bottom Field that our new fence has started to fall down! It is sliding into the stream!'

Then came the sound of the tractor starting up. Jack and Susan left Ben and Rosy in the stable and ran to see what was happening. The rain had made the ground muddy and slippery.

But Toby the tractor looked as bright and as cheerful as ever! By the time Jack and Susan reached Bottom Field, he was already lifting the pieces of fence out of the stream!

Each piece was loaded carefully into the farm trailer. Then, Farmer West hooked the trailer to the back of the tractor. Everyone looked very pleased. Jack and Susan felt like cheering!

Then, Farmer West got back into the driving seat and started up the engine. Toby the tractor made a lot of noise as he tried to pull the heavy trailer. His wheels spun round in the muddy ground.

Toby tried to go forwards, but he could not
move! The more his wheels spun round, the
deeper he sank into the mud.
'Drat!' cried Farmer West. 'Now, what can
we do?'

Just then, there came the sound of plodding
hooves from the old stables.
'Ben and Rosy!' cried Susan.
'Ben and Rosy!' cried Jack. 'They can pull
the tractor out of the mud!'

Ben and Rosy were led to Bottom Field. Soon, their big strong hooves were plodding slowly across the soggy, muddy ground as they made their way towards Toby the tractor.

They could see that Toby was very pleased to see them! Farmer West worked quickly to fasten their harness firmly to the front of the tractor. 'Over to you, Ben and Rosy!' he said. 'Pull!'

Ben and Rosy pulled hard. In no time at all, they had pulled the tractor, the heavy trailer and all the pieces of fencing out of the muddy ground and onto dry land!

This time, Jack and Susan really did cheer!
'Good old Ben and Rosy! We still need
them to work on our farm!' Toby winked his
headlights to show that he quite agreed.

Lady and Rover

Every day, Rover, the friendly sheep-dog at Buttercup Farm, waited at the gate to see his friend, Lady. She was a splendid white poodle, with a smart collar and a ribbon bow tied on top of her head. Lady lived in a big white house at the end of the lane.

As soon as Rover saw Lady, his tail began
to wag and he gave a friendly bark. 'Woof!
Hello, Lady! I have been waiting for you!'
Lady was always pleased to see Rover.

Sooner or later, there always came a sharp voice. 'Lady! Come here! You will get your feet wet!' Or – 'Just look at your lovely, woolly coat! It is COVERED in mud!'

Really, Lady only had a few splashes of mud. But Miss Fox, the lady she lived with, was always fussing about her dog. She did not like Lady getting in a mess!

Rover was looking forward to seeing Lady
in the big parade at the Dog Show! With
her ribbons and pretty bows, he was sure
she would win first prize!

And Rover? He was going to be in the Sheep-Dog Competition, showing everyone how well he could round up sheep and put them safely into the pen.

Tim, the shepherd, had trained Rover since he was a puppy. He only had to use his whistle and Rover knew what to do. It was a special whistle that only dogs can hear.

As the day of the Dog Show got nearer, the more Lady was brushed and groomed and fussed over. 'You are sure to win first prize!' smiled Miss Fox. 'I shall be SO proud of you!'

Even on the day of the Dog Show, Miss Fox kept brushing Lady's coat and polishing her little claws. Lady did not like it very much. She wanted to see her friend, Rover.

Soon it was time for Lady and Miss Fox to parade in the show ring. 'Hold your head up high, Lady!' said Miss Fox. 'Let the judges see what a pretty dog you are!'

People who were watching began to clap. 'What a lovely dog!' said one lady to her friend. 'I do hope the judges choose her. She deserves to win the prize!'

And in another field, Rover was also doing well! He had rounded up a flock of sheep and got them all together. Now all he had to do was to get them into the pen.

Tim blew his whistle as a signal for Rover. But, in the show ring, Lady heard it too! She knew that sound very well! It was Tim whistling for Rover!

Miss Fox felt Lady pulling at her lead.
'Stop, Lady!' she cried. 'Be a good girl!'
Tim blew his whistle again. This time, Lady gave a loud bark. She tugged at her lead more strongly.

Then Lady stood on her back legs and pawed at the air. That was the sound of Rover's whistle! Miss Fox could not hear it, but Lady could! She knew that her friend was somewhere near.

'Stop, Lady!' cried poor Miss Fox. But it was no good. Lady pulled so hard at her lead, she pulled Miss Fox over, right into the mud! 'Oh, no!' she moaned. 'Look at my lovely, new suit!'

But that was not all. Lady was running into the next field, mud and clumps of grass flying everywhere! She looked around for Rover, but all she could see was a whole lot of sheep!

Lady ran around the sheep, first one way, and then the other, just as she had watched Rover doing. Before long, she had got all the sheep into a tidy little group.

'Oh, no!' cried Miss Fox again, so loudly that everyone could hear. 'Just look at my beautiful poodle, Lady! She is dirty, she is muddy, she is untidy, she – she ...'

'She has just rounded up all those sheep and got them safely into the pen!' said Tim with a grin.

'Without anyone training her, too! What a clever dog she is!' said someone else.

'Winner of the beginner class in the Sheep-Dog Competition!' boomed the voice of a judge. 'But I do not have the name of this poodle! What is she called? Who does she belong to?'

'She belongs to me!' cried Miss Fox. Now, she sounded very proud indeed! 'And her name is Lady!'

Then everyone began clapping and cheering all over again.

Tim led Rover across to see Lady. The two friends rubbed noses and wagged their tails. They were both so pleased to win a prize! As for Tim and Miss Fox, they started talking.

Lady is still a splendid white poodle, with pretty ribbons and a bow on top of her head. And Rover is still a hard-working sheep-dog with mud on his paws.

But Miss Fox does not bother so much about Lady getting her feet wet. Lady and Rover are together nearly all the time. And so are Tim and Miss Fox!

Shawna Sheep

Farmer Nancy was proud of her sheep. Their wool was the finest that anyone had ever seen. The sheep with the best wool was Shawna. 'My wool is so soft!' she kept saying. 'People only come to Farmer Nancy to buy wool because I am here!'

One day, Shawna saw a lady and a man looking at all the other sheep in the meadow. Farmer Nancy was there too. 'Shawna!' she cried. 'I was just coming to find you!'

'Meet Kate and Bill!' said Farmer Nancy.
'They are going to spin wool this year at the
summer fair!'
'And it is your wool we want to spin!' said
Bill. 'Such fine, soft wool!'

This made Shawna feel very proud! Off she went in a smart trailer with Farmer Nancy, looking very grand! The day was fine and warm and she felt rather hot. But that did not matter!

There was a crowd waiting to see Shawna at the fair! Farmer Nancy took some wisps of wool from her fleece and Bill began to spin them into a long thread on his spinning wheel.

'This wool will be made into a lovely, soft scarf!' Kate told the crowd. 'It is the finest, softest wool that anyone can buy!' After that, everyone wanted to pet Shawna and feel her wool.

Shawna soon felt very hot indeed! But she tried not to mind. 'You are quite a famous sheep, Shawna!' said Farmer Nancy. 'But I am sure you will be glad when shearing begins tomorrow!'

'What is shearing?' said Shawna. But Farmer Nancy did not hear. Shawna had to wait until she was back at the farm. She went to see the other sheep.

'What is shearing?' she asked them.

'It's when you feel cooler!' said one.
'And lighter!' said another.
'And smaller!' added a third sheep.
'Cooler?' bleated Shawna. 'Lighter?
Smaller? But, what IS shearing?'

'Don't you know?' another sheep bleated back. 'Shearing is when you lose your thick, woolly coat!'
And off they went, bleating in delight at the look of shock on Shawna's face.

'N-no!' she cried. 'Not my lovely, soft wool?' But it was true. Next day, the shearers were busy peeling away the wool from each sheep. How bare they all looked afterwards!

They skipped and jumped around, feeling so light and so cool in the warm sunshine! But Shawna's mouth was wide open in horror. She did not want to lose her soft, fine wool!

Off she ran, feeling so very hot! She was glad to rest in the shade of a big tree. But, as the sun rose higher, the shadow of the tree became shorter, until there was no shade at all!

Feeling even hotter, Shawna ran into the
dairy, where butter and cheese were made.
There were tiles on the walls and on the
floor, smooth and cool. Shawna began to
feel better.

Then, a strong hand pushed her from behind. 'Out you go, Shawna!' said the dairyman. 'Today is shearing day! Time to lose your woolly coat!' And he pushed her out of the door!

Off she ran again until she came to a stream. Shawna put her feet into the cool water. 'That is better!' she said. 'I was feeling SO hot!' Still the sun beat down on her woolly back.

Then Shawna had another shock. It was Sam, the sheep-dog! 'Woof! Woof!' he barked. 'So here you are, Shawna! Farmer Nancy says you must come and get sheared!'

'I WILL not lose my fine, soft wool!' bleated Shawna. 'I will NOT!' And off she ran. But Sam could run faster. He darted in front so that she could go no further. Then Shawna had an idea.

There was a wire fence around the field. Shawna began to squeeze under it. Sam, the sheep-dog, could not follow her now! Suddenly, she felt a strong tug at her coat. What had happened?

'Baa!' bleated Shawna. Had Sam taken hold of her wool in his strong teeth? She tried to pull free.

'Woof!' barked Sam. 'You have caught your coat on the wire, Shawna!'

Sam ran to fetch Farmer Nancy. 'Hold still, Shawna!' she said. 'Let me try to cut you free. Then you can come and have your fleece sheared properly! You silly old sheep!'

By now, Shawna was too tired and much too hot to do anything! All the other sheep were skipping about and enjoying the sunshine. They looked so cool without their thick woolly coats.

The shearer soon cut away Shawna's fine, soft wool!

'It's a shame about the big hole in your fleece,' he said. 'That is where you caught your wool on the wire fence!' Poor Shawna!

But, she had to admit, she did feel very nice and cool! Then, Bill spun lots of woolly thread on his spinning wheel, ready for Kate to weave into beautiful scarves and shawls!

Their work won first prize at the town craft fair! 'Fine, soft sheep's wool makes beautiful things,' said Kate. And Shawna, standing in her pen beside Farmer Nancy, quite agreed!